SAN DIEGO    AUSTIN    ORLANDO

GULLIVER
BOOKS
HARCOURT
BRACE
JOVANOVICH

# THE CHINESE MIRROR

ADAPTED FROM
A KOREAN FOLKTALE BY

MIRRA
GINSBURG

ILLUSTRATED BY

MARGOT
ZEMACH

*Library of Congress Cataloging-in-Publication Data*
*Ginsburg, Mirra.*
*The Chinese mirror.*
*"Gulliver books."*
*Summary: A retelling of a traditional Korean tale*
*in which a mirror brought from China causes confusion*
*within a family as each member looks in it and sees a*
*different stranger.*
*[1. Folklore—Korea]   I. Zemach, Margot, ill.*
*II. Title.*
*PZ8.1.G455Ch   1987   398.2'7'09519   [E]   86-22940*

ISBN 0-15-332877-0     (Library: 10 different titles)
ISBN 0-15-332914-9     (Single title, 4 copies)
ISBN 0-15-332974-2     (Replacement single copy)

*Printed in the United States of America*

TO GRETA, MAYA, AND MARK

— M.G.


FOR ODETTE

— M.Z.

There was a time, long, long ago, when no one in our village had ever seen a mirror. One day a villager went on a distant journey, all the way to China.

There, he went into a store and saw a strange round shiny thing. He looked at it, and a man's face looked back at him. He smiled, and the man smiled back at him. He stuck out his tongue, and the man stuck out his tongue. "Sell it to me," he said to the storekeeper. And he brought the mirror home with him.

At home he hid the mirror in a trunk, afraid its magic might be lost if everybody saw it. Once in a while he'd take it out secretly, laugh with pleasure, and then hide it again.

"Why is he laughing when there is nothing to laugh at?" his wife wondered, and began to watch him. One morning she saw him take a small round shiny thing out of the trunk, look into it, and smile. When he went out, she took the mirror and glanced into it.

"Oh, oh!" she cried.
"The cruel, faithless man!"
And she ran to her
mother-in-law, wailing,
"My faithless husband,
your son, brought home
a pretty, young wife from
China, and keeps her
hidden in the trunk. Look
at her, there she is!"

"Stop wailing," said
her mother-in-law, "and
let me see the young
beauty."

She glanced into the mirror, and burst out laughing. "My son may not be very clever," she said. "But why would he bring home a wrinkled old crone? No, there must be something else to it. He'd never get himself such a wife, it's just your foolish jealousy."

At that moment the man's father walked in
and wondered why his daughter-in-law was crying
and his wife laughing.

"Let me see for myself," he said.

He looked, and shrugged his shoulders, and said,
"You sillies. This is not a woman, either young or old.
It is our neighbor's grandpa, with his
bald head and gray beard."

They kept looking and looking. But the young wife kept seeing a pretty young woman. The old woman kept seeing a wrinkled old crone. The old man kept seeing the neighbor's grandpa.

And none could convince the others
that they were wrong.

They put the mirror back in the trunk, still arguing.

Now, the man and his wife had a little son.

"What are they arguing about?"

he asked himself. "Let me see."

When they were all gone, he took the mirror and looked in, and saw a boy with a nice round pebble in his hand.

"Oh, oh!" he yelled. "The nasty brat stole my pebble!"

A neighbor happened to be passing by.

"Why are you crying?" he asked.

"Who stole your pebble?"

The boy held out the mirror and the man looked into it.

"You big fat bully," he shouted.

"How dare you hurt little children?"

He banged his fist into the bully's face. Out flew the mirror, crashed against the wall, and scattered into a hundred shiny splinters.

And that was the end of the stranger who
looked at the traveler, the young beauty from China,
the wrinkled old crone, the neighbor's grandpa,
the nasty brat who stole pebbles, and the
big fat bully who hurt little boys.

*The illustrations in this book were inspired
by the paintings of two eighteenth-century
Korean genre painters,
Sin Yun-bok and Kim Hong-do.*

*The illustrations in this book were done in watercolor on Crescent illustration board.*

*Designed by Joy Chu*

A 9
B 0
C 1
D 2
E 3
F 4
G 5
H 6
I 7
J 8